Love Without a NET...

Catch Me When I Fall, Pick Myself Up to Start All Over Again

Karen Ligon

PUBLiSH AMERiCA

PublishAmerica
Baltimore

Rickie —
Thank you
So much for
your support!
Love
Karen

ISBN: 1-4241-1771-2
PUBLISHED BY PUBLISHAMERICA, LLLP
www.publishamerica.com
Baltimore

Printed in the United States of America

Dedication

So many thoughts lay in my head.

I would like to dedicate this book "Love without a Net" to my sisters Audrey and Rosemarie, my daughter Shaunte, my mother and grandmother and my many girlfriends both old and new for inspirational lives, strength and endurance. Thank you for allowing me to share my stories and your stories that are blended into my poems.

To: Mark, Lucien (LJ) and Kyle for showing me their love and compassion.

And to my soul that holds deep memories and rich endless thoughts of Love and heartbreak.

Love, Peace and Many Blessings
Karen

Acknowledgments

I would like to take this time to thank my dear friend and fantastic artist, Mark S. Newland for designing the cover of my debut book "Love Is A Splendorous Thing with Many Assumptions" and for giving the public another chance to review his phenomenal work by designing the cover to this book. I thank you Mark for all of your support and grand gestures and for allowing our collaboration with your art meeting my poetry. You knew just how to make my work come alive!

You are my Artman! To continued partnership.

Love,
Karen

Table of Contents

I am not a poet 11
Love, Peace and Blessings 12
Just a Notion 14
Audrey and Rosemarie 16
Our Secret 18
Not Think of Me 19
And So It Is Over 21
Here I am Again 23
This Train is Leaving the Station 25
And So We Lay 27
Are You... 29
Jazz 30
I Have to Love You From a Distance 31
Others 32
I Am Not a Stalker 34
Sharpened Pencils 35
You are Lovely 36
InDifference 38
You Should Have Remembered 39
King Treated 41
Tugged 42
She Will Always Love You 43
I Dream of You 44
Smooth Love 45
Why Not Respond? 46
The Anticipated Stroke 48
How Do We Change Us? 50
Just Like That You Walked 51
Thinking 53
The Revision 55
Cried a Little 56
Then What Happens? 58
I've Been in REM 60

Check Yourself   61
Recognized   63
Too Late   65
My Observation of: The Bridges of Madison County
                                                        67
The Succession of Time   69
Security   71
Blue Moon   72
Full Moon   73
Dear John or Joe or Pete or Fill in the Blank   74
In the Middle   76
I Sing Anyway   77
So I Called You   78
Hi   80
Corner Turned   82
Untitled   84
Dress Me in Blue   86
Changes   87
My Second Chance With You   88
Please Make it Stop!!!   90
Untitled   91
Untitled   92
Once   94
Wedding Vows   96
Untitled   97
The Greener Grass   99
Fallen   101
I Thought You Were a Sheep   102
Unexpected   104
I Challenge You   106
Your New Woman Said I Rolled My Eyes at Her
                                                       107
Step Forward, Move Back   108
On My Knees   109
Full Libra   110

Mr. Boulder-Dash   111
Extra Credit   113
No Excuses   114
Deficient   115
We Will Never Be Friends   116
In the Car   118
If You Loved Me   120
Crazy, Crazy   122
Did You Find Someone New?   123
Porridge   124
Red Snapper   126
Cool   128
Happy Birthday   130
Wake Me   131
Where is the Love Letter?   133
Polaris   134
And So I Go   136

I Am Not a Poet

I am not a poet,
I write,
I write my feelings,
I tell my stories,
Things that I see,
A sort of step by step guide
A manual of me,
My thoughts are often jumbled, so I put pen to paper,
Anyone can do it.
It takes no special talent
Other than an overworked imagination
A too romantic notion,
Dreams that do not come true
And you could be writing as well.
My missteps,
My lost loves,
My never loves,
My under developed life,
My frankness,
My willingness to expose my inners
To show my personal self,
So I glide my pen across the paper
And express my issues,
My visions,
I must do this you see,
It is who I am.
Please do not call me a poet
For poets are well versed in prose,
Similes and metaphors,
But not me I am neither smart nor witty.
If one is looking for a poet, there is;
Nikki, Maya, Silvia and of course Shakespeare.
I am not a poet.
I just write.

Love, Peace and Blessings

I wish you…Love, Peace and Blessings
Although we are history,
And I daydream of you relentlessly,
wanting you to be part of my audience, my stage,
part of my existence,
any part, a little part
Wishing you could be with me.

I want to stroke you and for you to caress me,
Consume sunsets and sunrises,
For us to plan potential endeavors, together.
I wish you…Love, Peace and many blessings

And I know you have twisted away, turned a corner
and told me that you can't, won't be with me,
right now,
Although I am miserable, distressed and I feel discarded
I appreciate that it is difficult for you to be with me,
as it is excruciating for me to be without you.
for there would be too much touching,
too much talking, too much of a connection,
too uncontainable and you forbid that.
We are too electric
and Air engages fire
and we could combust
We are chemically coupled indefinitely
jointly we ignite,
detonate
enthusiasm flamed
I wish you, Love, Peace and Blessings

I still love you, want you and wish you softness,
just to be with you would be brilliantly satisfying.
to be with you would unquestionably end my woe,
but you are honorable, guarded
and I must respect your feelings
and although I can not encompass you,
Please have extraordinary sunrises
and delicious sunsets
and lots of Love, Peace and many blessings.

Just a Notion

Perhaps there is only one person
for each and every one of us,
If that is true and we all
had one mysterious soul mate,
then might you be obliged
to the overall possibility,
that most are not with theirs.

Please bear with my thoughts
allow me to follow through
for it is my belief
that if there is only one,
one person for you and me
then how likely it could be
that we missed the exact time,
the exact place and exact state of mind,
where our soul mate might appear.

Not sure you comprehend?
well, allow me to attempt
an overworked explanation
Make clear these thoughts in my cranium.

Okay, we say our vows
and speak of undying love,
we consume all the passion and
indeed some compassion,
as we don our white gloves.

We meet in our high schools
and then continue with this puppy love.
We stride on the path of least resistance
staying away from the unknown and unstamped,
how rarely do we follow our instincts
or the red flags in our heads
How rarely do we just go with our feelings.
And so, we marry the ones that we are supposed to marry
the ones classified as very stable,
the ones our mothers love.

Now we must consider the offspring,
The ones we should have
and as we ponder the clear water we started with
becomes a bit murky,
then suddenly, well it's too late...
to ask yourself...
is this my true mate?

Okay so are they your soul mate?
Hear me when I say
that it is highly possible they ain't
for if the theory is correct
and there is to me only one soul mate
statistics very truly must state
the probability of you being with the person
that was prepared precisely for you
is the individual you haven't met
If this displeases you, do not be alarmed
It is entirely possible...you have time yet

Audrey and Rosemarie

In slow motion, not unlike a movie picture or an old speaky…I remember,
Although memories were placed in a compartment,
Laid to rest, to slumber, but was always there.
Still there, still here in my mind.
Holding hands in church,
Trying to behave as eyes checked on us.
On an airplane, we together, smaller,
Sharing decadent treats, prepared and smuggled in by our mother.
Mango Trees and Billy goats tied up at daybreak.
The long drives like, Niagara Falls with potato chips and ginger snaps for snacks
Dividing Twinkies and Pop Tarts.
Peanut M&M's and running for Mr. Softy
Licking the drippings,
Ice cream cones and the city pool.
Plats both long and short,
Twist after washing our hair on Saturdays.
Learning Double Dutch in the driveway and the card game SPIT
Running home before the street lights snapped on!
Playing Spooky cutting my head, both of us screaming at the sight…
White patent leather go-go boots kicking…
Riding the bus to our grandmother's house
Our shared history of him, being broken and then repaired by her.
The Bronx Zoo, the Botanical Gardens, the subway and school shopping.
Italian ices and pizza from Nick's.

Always having to take me with her.
She is taking a ride on my brother's back.
A whole Barbie town in our bedroom that had three twin beds.
Dawn Dolls stolen.
Being surrounded by women, powerful teachings.
Teaching that were edged, ways that can not be removed, ways that are burned into our souls.
Wearing her clothes and the fight that ensued.
Me with a nasty attitude, they well liked.
First loves, only loves and sick loves.
Movies being told to me, movies my mother would not allow me to see.
Now I cannot remember whether I saw the movie or was it told to me
Vivid.
The Green Granada!
Secret joyrides, The Gospel Choir and Tremont Baptist Church'
I understand who we are and why we are still together
Through marriages,
Through separations,
Through death,
In spite of my friends,
We are sealed like cement,
Solid,
Rock hard,
In spite of, their judgments, my judgments
We are unbreakable.
Always cherished, truthful, honest with some brutality.
Connected by my mother,
Sisters without choice,
Friends to the very end.

Our Secret

He put sun tan lotion on my back
I remember with a shudder,
being controlled and a bit uncomfortable
but he insisted actually he persisted
and I obeyed
his hands neared my bottom
and moved as if approaching my breast
and inside my thighs.
Again I said thanks…
in the hopes for my release,
perhaps he might discontinue his descent,
but again he pursued,
and I to be respectful, I allowed him to touch me again
even with bile rising in my throat.
I looked into his eyes
eyes yellowed where it should have been white
me fourteen, he a man stepping rapidly towards fifty
and there it was, a pant…faint
not recognizable to the naive,
but hindsight I should have understood.
He came so close.
His breath was on my breath
Suddenly I moved and while my knees shook
I walked away and never, never, never
told a soul.

Not Think of Me

How dare you not think of me?
We were exceptional
Like a powerful romantic movie
Like The theater
The Opera
The ballet
The Rivera
The sunset
The sunrise
The Nile
The louve
We were "Somewhere in time"
"Pretty women"
"When Harry met Sally"
We were "Brown Sugar"
And we had the scent of love
You know…that almost love
Almost deep
Almost forever
Almost me plus you
A pair
Two shoes
Spoon and soup
Ice cream and cone
We could have been
But apparently you stopped thinking of me
I often wonder
How this could be,
Maybe you did not understand
That we were set up to be
Romeo and Juliet without death

Scarlet and Rhett
Frankie and Johnny
Me and you
Were you not there with me?
Did you not feel it?
Did you not know that you and me
Should be we
My name should be linked with yours
Maybe not man and wife
But those couples that are known
Linked to one another
Where the hell were you?
I thought we had a romance
I thought you "only had eyes for me"
I thought I sent you
That I was the Sunshine of your life
That I was your lady
Your everything
Your shining star
Your brick house
Your all Luther songs
That you "thought about me"
Your all and all
Obviously we were in different romances
Cause, no matter how I try
I can't forget

And So It is Over

So it is over and it should be
We both knew it was coming
That the curtains were drawing to a close
That the portly woman was about to sing her closing cry
We knew that we glimpsed the last of our togetherness
Tender thoughtfulness
And we saw the light...
Very dim at first then becoming brighter and brighter
We were transfixed
Knowing but not moving away
The credits are rolling and folks are leaving the theater
Dusk has eclipsed into Evening
Dark seeping under the doors
Last bit of sun backing away
Disappearing.
Admitting it was the issue,
Saying it out loud to make it true.
Lack of touching with a line drawn down the middle
Me off my soap box
Heart not in pain,
Gave the pain up once I forgot to care
Can we venture back?
Not to be...for love crept out slowly,
Almost unnoticed,
Attention unpaid,
No toll offered
No offering to the Gods.
I knew this would end,
It always ends
And as I sat waiting when I was happy
It still happened suddenly,

Almost by surprise.
The end tapped us on the shoulder and we barely turned to notice
And so now it is over and it should be

Here I am Again

Sunday, Sunny, Sandy and with water
Laying, tanning and thinking....
We just barely noticed each other
Not but a week has gone by
And here I am in my absolute preferred place
Thinking of you.
Inside of a week, not even a month
And I don't even know you
However it seems that I have made your acquaintance prior to
our meeting
Crazy!
or awesome, either, both.

And I contemplate, what will happen?
For I know something ought to.
I agonize about my thighs
My flawed body,
My breast...
My imperfections
And I know I shouldn't meander there
But who am I jesting...who doesn't,
Once attracted to
Be honest...fast forward to the first time
And I redden.
Will I be depreciated with one hard look?
Not be up to your standards...be minimized.
Not substantial once scrutinized...
And I am in sixth grade in a matter of minutes,
The too tall girl with thick pony tails....
Here I go again wondering, over thinking and making myself
nervous.
Will the connection be solid?

Or fragile like colored glass
And shatter, break into pieces.
Is what I am feeling real...basic?
This is me reflecting; Sunday, Sunny, Sandy and with water
As I feel the sand under my feet,
It is so difficult to consider that I am here
Thinking of you,
Wishing for completion,
Unsealing my heart,
Shedding the armor,
Almost hoping,
And day dreaming,
Again.

The Train is Leaving the Station

The ache has gone
heart still fully intact
In fact, I believe it is remarkable
that I am still breathing, I had not thought.
The abdominal pain seized,
it has subsided
Yielded.
No surgery required,
just a slow, slow process of rehabilitation
Steady, steady...steady with intense control
and some time added in-between.

They call this healing,
and so it goes,
My Mama told me this would happen,
just give it some time and the pain will fade.
You told me "this too shall pass"
and so it has passed. No it is passing, slowly.
Like a rain shower on a tropical island,
fierce while it has happened,
then the heat comes and you forget the rain.

As winter turns to spring
Spring to summer
Summer to autumn
Life positions me on a train,
but I took the local, so I made some stops along the way.
I keep looking for you to run along the tracks...
looking to get on, to get back to me.
I had hoped to see you running,
running to catch up to me.
I thought I might see you saddled on the white horse,

chasing me,
saying you made a mistake,
instead my heart has been bandaged...mended, but not undivided.
I progress forward reluctantly

And So We Lay...

After an effective climax
I wonder is this the end
Or the beginning of something regained

We are not new and shiny
Rather we are a bit tarnished
And worn
However, we do fit approximately,
We connect, we unite
After our coming together,
After my drought, your willingness
To go back to were we were before
To consume and be consumed
By wanting

You, with all your love for me
And I love you too,
But I need to flee
And I know that I will regret my departure
You hold on tightly to my loosening hand
Our fingers lock for a second
And I open mine first.

It would be easy to stay,
Stay where I am loved
To not enter into the unknown,
Where love may never find me again

For I am aging,
And the best of my crop has been harvested
To stay home would be peaceful,
And cowardly,

And I know I must go,
And I go after we lay,
Bending my head
Guilty and with love.

Are You...

Are you wondering about me?
I know that I am wondering about you!
Shit, I am too old to do this again.
This falling without a parachute
This love without a net,
Without a safety,
Just letting go
Recklessly.
Letting go,
Reaching for your hand.

Too many times before
I have been here
And now I have been
Flying solo
And here you strut
With this assurance,
This confidence.
Looking at me like that,
Going through me,
Right through me,
Too keen,
Too knowing
And I must stop and catch my breath
Straighten up my armor,
For I am afraid to be seen,
So reflections make me try to hide,
Hide from his eyes.
Shit I am too old for this,
But here I go,
without the net.

Jazz

Marion Meadow's performs.
His saxophone was actually singing,
On a clear midnight sapphire evening
And I sat back,
on a comfortable chair
With my best comrade
and nearly saw the melody
Descending through the air
The aroma of the grass sailing through the air
Margaritas jade.
White wine and delicate cheeses
savoring olives,
and oh so satisfying strawberries
And I closed my eyes
To utter thank you,
Thank you to God,
for my inner most delight
chasing away,
the lonely part of me,
hidden far away
imbedded,
deep inside of my soul
the soprano saxophonist speaking to me
revealing to me that I need not be searching
I just need to be here indefinitely.

I Have to Love You from a Distance

From Far, Far away…never have I felt so.
Unsure of my deal.
Rivers must gush between us,
Cities and States
Forest and gardens
Highways and country roads
There must be a Fort between you and me
With battle lines securely manned
Soldiers prepared for action
You I must Love from a distance
I wish it were not so,
But combustible we two
Together; fire
Together we explode
Air entices fire
Either to excite it or to blow it out,
Like a candle in the air can not stay lit
Or the raging flames that can not go out.
Fire takes the control
And others must come in to cool the flames
You take my control,
My will, my soul
I become inactive,
Controlled by you
Vulnerable and inadequate, perplexed and deprived
my knees weak and shaking and I lose senses
I am not strong, but wanting, so we must retire to different
sides,
The big sky must expand for miles between us two.

Others

It does not affect just me
there are many involved
too many to mention
too many to consider
so I venture on
precisely as I am
why you articulate
well
it does not affect just me
there is a matter of my reputation
and of course...
what is supposed to be
and least not forget
all the expectations
the desires of others
and other peoples dreams
dreams that I am part of
imaginings that I make come true
and of course
we must not upset the equilibrium
move things unequal
let things change, ever so slightly
or let possessions come crashing down
I am accountable
and courageous I am
Revolutionizing my life?
Not me!
see it doesn't just affect me
there are others
to speak of
others that care for me

honest
be honest
well then what happens?
there are attachments
and commitments
and comings
and going by appearances
you can not require me to be happy
I have other things to ponder
after all my life
is not just about me

I Am Not a Stalker

we f—ked
at first, I did not think
but damn it,
that must have been it.
The thing is,
if that was so
Why not just attempt
and let me know
Why did you pretend
it was something it was not,
sending flowers and stuff,
taking me dancing,
and asking me about myself,
holding my hand,
and pretending to be concerned
sending me songs
and gazing in my eyes
cause then I became surprised
when all it was
was just a f—k
at least if you had just stated
that natural fact,
I might have agreed
and knew what it was about
damn you brothers and others
that don't get that shit...
I could have been down
had you just asked
but now I am hurt
cause you built it so high
and you wonder why
I keep calling your ass up

Sharpened Pencils

As I drove, I saw this absolutely perfect sky,
A crisp September day,
Autumn just creeping in,
The sharpened pencil feeling,
school is in session.
A new backpack, notebooks,
starting fresh.
And I felt safe,
in control,
and extremely happy.
then,
I did not believe it was happening...
I walked into a meeting,
as always planning a project,
checked my watch; 8:40.
I was busy admiring my new suit and fresh new shoes,
when the interruption came,
an interruption of my life, many lives.
A 747 crashed into a building,
New York, New York...
on a perfect September day,
when the sky was ice blue
and big puffy white clouds gathered unassuming in the sky,
and I stared unbelieving, with shock and horror,
surprised, bewildered,
it happened while I was in my perfect suit,
wearing shiny shoes,
dreaming of sharpen pencils

You Are Lovely

You are lovely,
Yes that is the declaration I summoned...
I deliberated long and hard
About words to describe you
And I came up with lovely,
You are lovely
Perhaps I could have used a different characterization,
Maybe a more polished word,
Vibrant and expressive,
But as I thought, lovely floated around my head
Stayed there and took up space,
Did not want to budge
Wanted to lay there
With all your attributes;
Tall
Dark,
Handsome,
Solid
Masculine,
Kind
Sexy,
Relevant,
For if you were not relevant,
I would not write of you,
But I digress...
Intelligent
Motivated,
Classy,
Mysterious
But I want to use lovely,
For lovely is to me a word with a feeling attached

A word with love hidden inside
Or blatant,
But I can say lovely,
Before my lips could say love,
So this one is for you,
Because you are lovely

Indifference

I stare at the spot
in the ceiling
while it goes on
I admire the pattern on the ceiling
I glare at the window
while it is taking place
I examine the pattern of the panes
I review my day to come
while it goes on
I decide where I should eat for lunch
I think of my children
while it is supposed to be...
I think of my children
It is amazing that one does not notice
that I stare at the ceiling
glare at the window
Contemplate eating
and think of my children
while it is happening
it's a wonder
but, I will continue
to look at the ceiling
imagine what the day will bring
decide on my dressing
and what dinner should be
all while it is happening to me

You Should Have Remembered

Always missed once gone
While
I was there, I was
Unnoticed
and then
you can't seem
to get over me
but, you had numerous chances
chances to state
your feelings
your emotions
your views
others noticed me
how they noticed me
while with
you didn't think to take a second look
to invite me into you
While we were together
never a compliment
passing by your perfect lips
never a proud moment
now I hear about how you felt
then
you were too removed to tell me then
and
I told you that you would be sorry
you did not
believe
and now you cry to your friends
you feel abandon
but

you brought this to you
you forgot
to do the things you should know
and I hope for you
and might I add,
your next love
you will remember
not to forget.

King Treated

require to be treated well
desire me to respect you
feel you are gallant
Possible nobility
You are the man
Looking for service
And sacrifices
Bath your feet with perfumes
Run your water
And make your meals
Be there for you
whenever you are ready
have your children
and clean your house
be your sounding board
must be beautiful
good mother
and sex goddess
be quiet and passive
yet communicate well
Entertain you
and stay home
while you go out
meet and greet
I should have a smile when you return
and never ask where you have been
no right to
because you want to be treated like a King
and all these things
I promised to do,
do when I am treated like a QUEEN.

Tugged

Short-end
It is like drawing straws
and getting the short one
It is a joke of sorts
because always
wanted to walk that walk
and have a Pickett fence
what happens when your dreams come true?
and you have precisely what you imagined.
the learned desires
the supposed to stuff
well for many
it is exactly as it should be
but there are those
who feel that they got the short-end.

She Will Always Love You

don't be fooled
she will always belong to you
she will go her separate way
but she will always be yours, always
Oh she will see others
and she will dance the dance
even tango
she will follow her dreams
and marry
and she will raise children
that will be successful
and she will travel the world
and have a wonderful life
but she will always love you
for you can't fight with your heart
it never forgets the love
the love you try to place in a box
is always first
so you should go and run
and follow your dreams
because she will always love you

I Dream of You

I dream of you every night
I never will forget
your face
your lips
your tone
every night I dream of you
I try not to
but you are etched
in my mind
I love you still
although it seems
so long ago
like a lifetime has passed
you are in my daydreams
I want to touch you
for you to touch me
feeling the sheer mist of your breath
on my back
and rotating around
and around
every night I dream
Spectacular
Erotic
Explicit
Unduplicated dreams
I pray to not remember
cause, I can't truly move passed
when you are presently in my mind
so connected to my future
so I live in a fantasy
of us together,
dreaming always of you

Smooth Love

I Love you
for all that is bad in it
because I am comfortable
and contented
and you know me
and I know you
and it is familiar
and unhurried
and we are developed
and we share history

I love you because it is you and me
because we are one
because we are connected
like screws needing to be bolted
to stay connected

I love you
because you charm me everyday
and you care
because you take care of me
and I always know what you want

I love you
because we are committed
we share the same views
you make me smile
you make me laugh

I love you because
it is not easy
but because you are worth the sometimes bumpy ride
as long as we are driving together.

Why Not Respond

it would be mature
but I presume
that may be
too much to ask of you

I tried to connect
again
again I tried to connect
but I deduce
that was too much to anticipate

my recollections are not
that unfocused
Well, maybe iced and
a bit sweetened
but I've been so gracious
at least you could say hello

I pause again for you
to perhaps counter
but I wait in vain
for there is no intension
from you to me

and I wonder, why?
was it less than I imagined
or more than I imagined
this caused me much woe
and I questioned my judgment

might I make a suggestion
even if it doesn't give you
much in the way of pleasure
if you would just make a response
perhaps we both could but this to rest

For it is a coward
that will not stand tall
and I hope that you are
not that person after all

The Anticipated Stroke

I knew I'd shoulder the burden
but I let you, and I knew
I knew, oh how I knew
I tried to stay away
I ran and evaded
I spied from a peculiar distance
because I knew
what would come to pass
if we moved nearer
I was a fugitive
for what appeared to me, to have been a lengthy time
stirring slowly like a tigress
hesitant of her prey
screening you viewing me
and I crept gradually
side eyes exploratory
a slight memory in my thighs
a flashing of hot water running,
cascading down
a ruddy sensation seeped through my veins
knowing from the look in both of our eyes
the electric shock that I felt when we shook hands
irreversible tracks...leading me from to
I remembered what I thought I had forgotten
I side stepped
because I knew
that your touch
would change my life
I did not stare directly
not directly in your eyes
I was in crisis,

needed a lifeline,
I started to slip
crossed
and doubled back
and watched you stark
and then it happened
and I lost restraint and
the after affect of your touch will linger everlastingly
always in my head,
for you were never again
never, ever again in my bed

How Do We Change Us?

Bring the stars back into common skies
Make us long for a known embrace
Catch the moonlight in our eyes
Allow us to desire one another's face
We seemed to be prepared for the forever
How do we make it better than just alright?
How do we become less than complacent?
Make it like it prior to us knowing each other so well
or should I say too well
Have we lost the intensity?
the challenge for a new day
the sparkle that we once were
the charming of each other's soul
can we warm a home?
without the kindling
do we want to or do we ride and make no sudden moves
how do we change us?
who we have become
or do we just exist without any expectations
you tell me.

Just Like That, You Walked

Out of his head
just like that
one pop
and he was gone
just like that
I turned away
and he flew
as I talked
and told
my stories
not waiting for
him to respond
he walked away
just stepped
I had
more
more to tell
now he won't
know
cause just like
that
he climbed out
was I not perceptive,
to his imperfection?
but I was talking
talking to him
telling him
my me stories
my history
my dreams
and
oh my goals

was I not listening?
Gosh
maybe I
forgot
to be attentive
maybe too assertive
Demanding?
Why?
Was I revealing too much
no longer a mystery
Well
he did not
talk back
I am left
left with the
what did I do?
was it something
something I said
He vanished
can't get
in touch
no response again
and again
I think he
just
up and left
only
I
require
Explanation
he just
finished.

Thinking

How do you recognize what you know?
Distinguish what you see?
Go right through me
Viewing me from within
Seeing what I shield so well from others.
After our conversation
I am in a fog, a self induced haze
Thinking,
A memory of a song played
The meaning,
Sinking deep within my soul
Talking...
Pure intuition,
How?
Can it just be physical?
Or is it an essential,
Thinking,
Contemplating,
The lyrics and melody,
you played for me
And I felt it
In between my legs
Becoming active
What has been dormant
Awaking,
Living again,
From you just knowing,
Me.
I am intrigued,
Mystified, enthralled
Geared up.

Even if it's just an instant
If it is a passing summer breeze
Right now I am captivated
Standing at attention
Willing to ensue

The Revision

A slight alteration,
Not to be noticed by the outsiders,
The ones not acquainted with the atmosphere,
A shift in the temperature ever so slightly,
I was fascinated with you,
Unexpectedly, but you have always been
in the adventure that is my life,
but with a gentle wind
I was focused and you were different
glistening and reflective
a sudden apparition.
you connected to a missing link,
not to be helped, I watched
paid closer consideration
There are particulars that were once disregarded
your intensity,
your excellence,
your exhilaration
The erotic
The toxic
the invitation
my imagination leapt
I went right there.
I wanted to RSVP
However, won't be in this lifetime
but maybe next time
we could complete this round
this unpredictable event
this astonishing magnetism can be accomplished
the circle could end with a slight change in perception
this unpredictable ocean could be placid
we could ride on a solar wind
and be happy or perhaps not.

Cried a Little

But why do I lie
I cried buckets
I remembered when
and cried some more

I longed for
and hoped for and
wished upon a star,
the moon
a cloud
I prayed
and answered e-mails that said
if I did, my wish would come true
still it did not
so I cried
and cried
and filled pots and pans with tears
striped faced
and water stained eyes
with dark half moons
and nothing could hide
oh how I cried

I tried not to
but still they came falling
and you said it was weak
yet I cried
I felt hollow
empty
and could not have believed
that here I stand

without a tear
no tears ready
I still long for
and wish on stars
and the moon
I still remember
and I am reminded
I still miss
I still want
but no more crying
just an uncorrectable broken heart

Then What Happens

after falling apart
after the crying
after a bit of you have disappeared
after the words you said
become untrue
Me, unable to breath
and can not touch a morsel

What happens then...?
after wishing for run-ins
and waiting by the phone
and hearing silent ringing
and making up scenes
creating excuses for bad behavior
saying it is your allergies,
when you know you can't stand up straight
because of heartache

Then what happens...?
after replaying the memories
and hoping that you would change your mind
and return for a minute, a second.
After all tears have fallen
and pieces are forever gone

Then what happens...?
something enters you
and you know,
Never again
and you miss something
but it will never return

because you are no longer naïve
you know the next one will come
and you will get back on the horse
but never so freely,
for the pain is still there
and you recognize that at any time
you could be
in the "then what happens"
Again.

I've Been in REM

Rapid eye movement:
REM: Definition: active period during which dreaming
occurs
Living inside my dreams
Not waking
taking cover under the covers
living in REM
rapid eye movement
sleeping
this is my phenomenon
sleep is a complex activity
with me, with us all
and even though
The activity consumes one-third of our lifetimes
and can overpower all other needs.
I have been living in REM
dreaming
never deeply sleeping
memories always close
and painful
overwhelming
not resting, never rested
in the REM stage
in my life.
the brain is very active
I walk in my sleep
I talk in my sleep
I prepare meals in my sleep
I am asleep
I am in REM
Rapid eye movement

Check Yourself

Double check
and look side ways
across the walk
across the street
and keep a
watch on your back
for she will get you,
when you are not watching
unspeaking
she will be unnoticed
for she remembers
remembers what you said
How you looked when you said what you said
Your touch
and your smell
and that she was everything,
your everything
and she will tell her friends
that you said what you said
you did what you did
you went where you went
that she was your girl
so double check
and watch your step
while you are out
working on new endeavors
creating new lives
redeveloping your personality
your history
erasing her from your chalkboard
making her not part of your past

be careful
for the hurt will come,
and come, when least expected
stop showing out
and hanging out
watch
wait and see
for it may not be her that gets you
it just might be me.

Recognized

Will you experience me when you see me?
Was I essential in your significant ones?
You made my record.
Did I make yours?
Will you recognize the importance?
the necessity that you became,
or is that just how I will have appreciation for you
I take for granted that my feelings are relative.
your importance to me,
depends on my significance to you
I speculate
if what I seek
is real, was real
or was I dreaming
for there was such a Hit or miss,
perhaps, I missed the mark all together
never being a good shot,
a profound player.
I was the one picked last
the weird one,
the girl too lofty,
too bizarre
or too intense,
was I not your amazing?
Although you were mine.
not enough something
and too much something.
the one with the scars
and the confidence.
so I am unsure
not quite stable with my thoughts

my core
our coalition
how it developed
did it happen as I thought
as I remembered
or was I misled
or did I confuse
I guess that depends
on if I am recognized

Too Late

Don't go changing now...
when I wanted you to peek within
and observe what could have been rearranged
you would not hear of any such change

So here you come progressing
with a new-fangled approach
a innovative view, a pep when you pace
and a fresh way of talking
now you want to have a metamorphosis
Don't go changing now

I was trying to tell you about you
and how you connected with me
and my feelings
I would become frustrated,
but what did that matter,
you insisted and persisted on doing you
whether being truly you was wrong or right
you did what you felt was best
for you, and not the team,
So don't go changing now

It doesn't help to reminisce
on how I was,
and where I was going,
and what you thought I should do,
be.
You claiming "how we fit"...before
because we definitely do not fit...anymore
So don't go changing now
Let me reiterate, I asked you many times

many times when I cared,
to consider or even contemplate,
what I meant to you
I wanted to compromise
and you…wouldn't even think of it
you did what you had to do. Never yielding
We were you, the after thought was me
I was there when you got tired of being on your own
when you remembered that you had someone at home.
So don't go changing now

I spoke…
I screamed
I threw things
trying to let you know,
that I was slipping
into the "never you mind" stage
Once in the stage, you never recover
I am out and you are still in
So don't go changing now
Not when I am so indifferent

My Observation of: The Bridges of Madison County

So why did she not leave?
Up for debate;
Yes.
Much later her children would find
Who she was
How she loved and choices she made
Never really becoming bigger
Or better, just there
Loved, but allowed her passion to leave in that truck,
On a dusty road...gone
Disregarding that her soul beckons her to flee
To go to him as she recognized that it was not fleeting
And then came the letters...he loved her his whole life time,
as she him in silence.
How fitting that the rain came,
That he never noticed her pain, her tears
Was she stronger than most, or weaker than the selfish?
I would have liked to see what happened if she got out of the
car
And ran to her love,
How she might have changed,
How imperfect timing could have brought her life joy.
She never saw the Bridges of Madison County,
Not until he took her
She fell in love
Four days
He magnetized her life
Put her love in the spotlight
Her existence
Faded.

Loyalty made her stay...
Sacrificing her own deep smile.
Always thinking of others.
Some will counter and say she was strong...
I say she was weak,
Not wanting to take the risk,
To run for love and exist without guilt
I wish I felt differently,
But my dear Francesca was a coward in my eyes

The Succession of Time

Hours extended to days
Days moved into weeks
Weeks turned into months
And so it has been a year

The year without you
And the holidays we might have spent
The seasons we might have viewed together
The memories we could have made

I have felt small
Ashamed and useless
Concerned with worries of
How you are, how you have become

Are you with another?
making new friends
moving on and developing plans
as the year has passed

Still, I honor you.
I built a pedestal and placed you there
And lived my life in this stage
Of what if it all went right

I can't shake my memories,
My mind will not let you loose
There has been no closure
There is to be no contact

I retreated
And waved the white flag
I surrendered…
Because you said "okay stop"

I stopped and time passed

Security

Wrap your arms around me securely and tightly
for with your arms around me
I know, I know
I know I can face this fight

I will walk up front and true
Unique with filled passion and longing
I walk with distinction
I walk with full faith
that knowing that I may return to you
that I am not alone
Knowing
Knowing
that with you I am home

I enter into the cold
with the memory of your embrace.
I will travel securely with strength
you have given me such great gifts

I dedicated this day to you
and wait for the night
where our shared embrace
will keep me alright

Your power funnels through me
and provides me with fuel
you energize me
excite me and make me whole

I always move forward knowing...

Blue Moon

Under the full moon of blue here I am once again thinking of you
Within my heart and soul I remember when we
shared this moon together
just us two.

The memory is true; here I am once again under the full moon of blue.
Always the same, always nothing new.
With the air pressed against my face, I grasp and
grasp for the feel of you
I go around in endless circles, but my thoughts
always return to you.

I am again under the full moon of blue longing for you.
I count the stars and find the north and hope
Yes I hope that wherever you are
You're looking up under the full moon of blue thinking of me.

Full Moon

Pallid
Unyielding
Enchanting
Romantic
deserted
presumptuous
yet unassuming
Magnificent
I assemble...
and wonder where you are?
Remembering
sharing the full moon with you
where
where are you?
white
solid
Alarmed
unmovable
full intense moon
bright
Bold
I am lonely
Where?
Why?
When?
I am here
All alone
Under the full moon
seeking you.

Dear John or Joe or Pete or Fill in the Blank

I am writing you the Dear John letter in reverse
Why?
Because the assumption is that the female persuasion is
The culprit of these heart breaking letters
These cruel and cowardly letters of heart destruction.
I pose a very different view…
I am here to state that such letters are indeed
in the head of our masculine set…
Are they ever written?
Do you here my thunderous laughter?
With a ha, ha, ha I state
Almost never.
I have been at the heartbreak end numerous times and here
is how it goes;
Dear Susan, Dear Amanda, Dear Karen
here is the letter you will never get
assume what you may assume and understand that you
should have expected nothing.
you got to close,
you nagged (cared)
requested too much time
I need more than one woman
Etc.
But all he did was kiss me; whisper I will see you later
and closed the door behind him.
When I did not hear from him in what seemed like weeks,
but was only days, I rounded up Audrey, Joan, Kim and Rosie.
We discussed my relations of the past few weeks
I pondered and considered what could have gone wrong.
Dear Karen, you may fill in the blanks

because rest assured I will not be telling you why it's over.
I waited and waited but still there was no call
Again I spoke to my friends, we discussed and dissected
and still came up late.
I contemplated with Wanda, Toni and Shaunte
but we still could not comprehend just what I have done
I retold the story to both my mother and father of our last days and
we came up with scenarios to great to falter.
Finally I called and called to ask you to explain
when you did not respond
I wrote you a note
note returned unopened I assumed that we were history,
but How could I know
you never wrote a note
No Dear Karen ever appeared
you could have taken pen to paper to help me understand.
At least then I might have my ending,
But nothing
No Dear Karen.

In the Middle

I lay just there
just there I lay
taking care to acknowledge
of the placid...
the length and the width
just me in-between
right there in the center
no inhibitions
alone with impure thoughts
me, in the middle
just there
alone and by myself
with no thoughts but my own
I am loosely in the mix
toes and hands comfortable
I am sane
alive and willing
just me alone
but never lonely
in the middle
not right aligned
nor on the left
I am center stage
and so okay
in the Victorian scents
puffy goosed down
flowery and feminine
silk and tucked
untrammeled
and neat
in the middle of my enormous
scented Bed.

I Sing Anyway

La, La, La and Fa, Fa, Fa
Unafraid of judgments
and the sideways looks
I know all the words
and adjust to the melody.
I shout
I shout
and yell it out loud
pretending not to see my friends,
with their shielded grins
I do not see strangers bashing elbows
I sing anyway
I completely lose the tone
and become lost in the tunes
I have never really made an effort to find the notes,
lost so long ago in my heart
I sing anyway
unconcerned and not ever miffed
that perhaps I shant
or like my friends say I can't
I sing, I sing, I sing
La, La, La and Fa, Fa, Fa
with bold confidence and unabashed emotions
never concerned about those passing
as they shake their heads
or the comments of...
"You are so brave"
to sing like that.
I put myself out there
but I can't help myself
so I sing anyway
Loudly, boldly and freely.

So I Called You...

And nothing!
You said nothing!
Did nothing!
Reacted with nothing!
And how I contemplated
deliberated, discussed and analyzed.
made many excuses,
to friends and foes
You had to think about it
I was too pushy
You were too scared,
but you felt the connection
well, you must have,
you had to feel it,
cause you made promises,
no you did not actually say it,
but we made plans for some part of the future,
you introduced me,
and people knew about me
you told tales about me
and made me feel unique
and yours and we were going to be something
So…I thought he must be sick
or maybe he could not contact me
for he was being held hostage,
he may be lying in a ditch
or he loved me so much it was unbearable to him,
so he backed off.
what an imagination,
or was it protection
or fantasy

so I finally called
and you did nothing
said nothing
felt nothing
and I heard my replacement...
she was in the background
and I guessed,
that you were telling her
about your future,
your dreams
and your destiny
only it was a rerun
And, she will be where I was
and she will finally call
after making excuses
Contemplating
And discussing
And telling her friends
And when she calls
You will say nothing.

Hi

I waited and waited
seconds turned into minutes
minutes became hours
hours became days
days became weeks
weeks became months
and months became a full year
Let me tell you how I spent that year.
I waited
That sums it up.
Now do not get this twisted
I lived during the year of waiting
In the beginning of my waiting it was difficult
all I did was think of you and me,
the magical connection
the must have of it all
I thought of how we met
and how it was
and how we would fight.
I remembered your touch
the seconds that connected
I bored my friends with
analogies
I apologized
and talked for hours about you
I changed my life
just in case you wanted to come back.
I changed my ways
actions.
I investigated and plotted
and contemplated ugly schemes

I talked to you in my mirror
and replayed the last time.
I planed projects...just to get my mind off of you,
but I thought of you with consistency.
and after all of that
when you finally contacted me
you just said HI!

Corner Turned

With that hi, things started to alter
who would have deliberated, an entire 365 days had passed
the transformation that I made
the changes in me, in me
I had lived in the fantasy of your return
oh, I was going to say scores of things
and I thought, if only he would make contact
"Oh Happy Day"
I would demonstrate to him what I am made of
how fervent I was
how malleable I was
how much I am
how much he made me
the birds would have a new song
and springtime would be endless
and all that I have built,
would become unyielding
down with the house of cards
straw or brushwood
for inhabitants to blow down or out,
but brick, sturdy and cement.
major Elements

I would become right
Fixed
All the love that I held would explode
and all the feeling of me, touching of me
would stop for the fantasy arrived,
for my memory of your touching was so strong
that all I did was close my eyes and I exploded
this all by myself, with you in my head

but then you contacted me
and all you said was hi,
and I turned the corner
and left all of you behind.

Untitled

Before I enter your touch again
Let me say what you have been to me thus far
Before we proceed to higher confessions,
I want you to know that your smile is like my sunshine
I blossom in your light
I develop with your touch
I grow

The roads we have crossed have been like twilight shining
We have shared dawn's light welcoming a brand new day.
You have touched, I have touched and we have arrived
unsurprised
I realize that I need, not want, need you by my side
To awake in your warmth
see night through yours arms
become a unit, me and you to become us

I never whirl in such a fashion
charmed by your words,
heated by your passions
You have awakened my being
released my soul
and it has made me better

You have entered my dreams,
Became my future.
You have taken me to elevated levels,
steadied my flow,
changed my perceptions,
and become my reality,
from which I can not return to the ordinary

you raised my expectations,
all along I knew mediocrity
but now I know glorious.

Dress Me in Blue

Dress me in blue
it would really suit
I am not to wear yellow, pink or purple
for those colors are for the happy people
which I am not
Dress me in blue for all my judgments
fears, and lack of imaginings
for the fading of my persona
the fabrication of me

If I were in blue
I would not have to feign
to be red, green or pastel pink some days
I would not have to pretend to be bursting
but I could just be without presumptions
remember no red for me for the implies fervor
and enthusiasm I am lacking

I have lost numerous gift boxes
I have introduced myself to so many hardships
for which I am the one to blame, no excuses
I have agreed too much
and taken too little
I am to be dressed in the color of blue

Changes

I felt a chill this morning
I knew it would be arriving soon
but as I walked swiftly
I realized that I was walking like winter

The sun was shining, and that was deceitful to me
for looking through my windows
it looked so inviting,
I assumed without knowing
your cold laughed ate me
I had to quicken my pace

Autumn was entering into our life
And our summer bowed out none to gracefully
and me too busy to notice the change

Your winter smile made me a fool

My Second Chance With You

At the beginning
I took you for granted, never really acknowledging your
sweetness
your endless passion for me,
your intelligence.
I overlooked you
how sorry I am.

with hindsight I know
I should have known better
I should have taken notice
more attention to your inner self,
I should have tried to be part of your soul,
and perhaps if I could have a do-over,
I might watch your eyes
examine your face
and know you.

It would seem that you've done your homework,
for you studied my actions
you knew my capabilities,
my wants
my needs and desires,
you know who I am trying to be, who I am.

And in the middle I thought I would die,
but I survived, you survived,
and we are still we,
it was so hard when you were you and I was me
separated and withdrawn.
I leaped to conclusions,

had I just paid attention,
I might have handled you better.

I stayed,
And I love you more than ever,
and I remember wishing I did not love you so much
and perhaps, I might have chosen an easier path,
but we are here…together,
putting the pieces back.

You can believe that this time I will pay closer attention
to those details so important,
your face,
your eyes
your silent moments,
your reflection of me in your eyes
your eyes when they are shining,
and weeping.
And I shall not take you for granted.

Please Make it Stop!!!

it is a sort of punishment
maybe for stepping out of the box
deep inside my heart
I am burning with desire
and a longing so far
I can not reach it
I think of him always.
Never forgetting,
always remembering
I love you!
I burn to the core
unable to find you
you are so clever,
quick.
You walked away
in the fucking middle.
I hate you for that
but not,
I miss you
it won't go away,
must have been real
come back
finish it!

Untitled

Love is wonderful if it suits
Is it ever, everlasting?
Often it is unattainable
Or just too hard to be kept

We forget those moments that
Were once shared
Forgotten moments of passion
We often move onward, forward towards the new

Fire, bodies engaged
Not longing for no other touch
Feeling like you could stare into each other
endlessly,
Stop!

The wood from the fire
Burns out slowly
And you try, and try, and really try
To relight the fire
You add flame starters
and more wood,
but the fire soon must go out.

The touch becomes familiar
Too familiar
And passions fly out the open window,
For it almost always is left open
And you are open to the new.

Untitled

Fly with me to where we could soar
I would love to see you beaming
with a rainbow beside your face
with just the right lighting
we will hold hands as we take flight.

I wish you could know
just what has been happening to me.

I wish I could read your thoughts,
you could enter mine,
we would know each others views
we could be as fresh as a new day in Spring.

Maybe we could talk about nothing important,
just thoughts, dreams, love
you could fill me with your ideas
and I could just listen, listen to your words.

Fly with me
forget reality
we must come back to it soon enough,
but for now hold onto me tight
and pretend we are the only two in the universe.

However a fool I may be
one could never say that I have never flown
when I look back, I will know that I took flight,
I took flight with you.
and what an incredible flight
what a sight to see

what laughter and joy will fill me
as I remember our flight,

If I could take you to the top
where I would stay
maybe someday you will soar higher and remember me
remember the girl who helped you to fly
and know that I was at my best...
when I started to fly...

Once

Once you looked
I looked back
Eyes met
We met
Each other
I did not know
Not really,
But you maintained.

Once you spoke
I took words from
Your lips,
I felt your
Words
It developed
It was known

Once we kissed,
We had to
Go further,
Right to the familiar,
We endured,
Actively
Pursuing the motion
We took off
The flight piloted by me
And now I need you constantly

Once familiar

You might be inaccessible
I might be accurate to access
That you will not be mine,
But now we will play
I will be the loser
But I will still remember
The once before.

Wedding Vows

I promise to Love, Honor and cherish.
It goes something like that I believe.
Here is how it should go...

I promise to forget your birthday
Anniversary
good days and bad days
I promise to not ask you about your days
And to tap when I need to release myself.
to never romance you
and you must work harder than any man
and come home and still be the housekeeper
the primary caregiver
maybe I will contribute financially,
but you should act as...
Bookkeeper
Dishwasher
The cleaners
Secretary
I promise to take you for granted,
Watch sports
Control the remote
have the children think that you are the evil one
cause all punishments must be dished out by you.
Wedding vows.

Untitled

You said that we would go to the sea
and venture to Venus
and take long walks
and view the foliage together
That I would meet your parents
and your children
your friends.

You told me we would see the movie...
You know the movie...
and that we would create memories
that we would grow into each other
that you were in love
and you claimed it as your own
asking me to say who it belonged to
you said my eyes were unlike anyone's you knew.

You shared your history
intimate details of who you were
your stories, your dreams
details you shared with me
you made me put you in my life
and that was just the first month.

I watched your eyes
they were truthful
I could not have known otherwise.
I took every utter and engraved them into my heart.

Then the earth moved,
or you met someone else

to which you properly said similar things to,
you were clever enough to change something I imagine

I am still here and you said you promised me nothing,
but you did...
maybe you did not say it, but you acted like it
and I like a fool believed you.
You made promises with your actions, your demands and
your passions.
It feels that I was just there to pass your time,
but you were indeed more than a fleeting relation, you were it.

The Greener Grass

I am trying to touch
longing
reaching out,
hard...
I want to feel the blades
touch the trees
Oak, Pine, Sycamore
smelling the maple in the making,
I try to taste
wishing
abiding
I want to run through, before the grass is shaped
Manicured, groomed.
while the grass is untamed and wild.
searching for wild flowers like daffodils
Reveling in the scent
bare feet against the length of the green.
I would place the blanket,
remove sweets from my basket
get fed with sweet fruit
and lay strength out on the greener side.
these are my imaginings...
but I am looking across,
uninvolved in the goings on.
I see all playing,
involved in games
picking and changing players
dancing and loving
The mower man comes to refresh and reshape,
to seed and water.
even though the grass is cut freshly,

so newly cut the scent
tickles my nose...
refresh my senses.
I long to walk on the fresh cut grass
feeling it through my toes.
I stand at my door
reaching out to touch
wanting to play...
with you on the greener side,
but I forget that you are looking
and longing to be on my side of the grass...

Fallen

I watched it fall
it started at dusk
then my moon appeared
stark and not blue
boom it appeared, just like that,
by the shining bulb
against the unnatural light
blowing sideways
I am inclined to reflect
on days of old
when I was a child
when I was brand new,
unopened.
new to love
I have watched this before
and waited impatiently for it to fall sideways
anxious
and come it did
crisply.
at dawn when I awoke
I would go to watch
and know the day will be absent of sunshine
and I liked that
no promises, able to stay indoors
not expected to be happy or cheery
and it falls sideways
against unnatural light
each one unique
special
shaped jagged
like me

I Thought You Were a Sheep

Why would you say such things?
when you know you would withdraw
without warning.
When you knew where I was,
because you brought me there
and don't say you didn't
cause you are the reason
the reason I am misinformed
about you and who you are
I thought you were something
but I am realizing that you are not what you should have been.
I upheld you—moved you
let you be something to me
and let you mean something to who I would be
you faked it, to obtain it
and lied without opening your mouth
you acted kindly, but you are not kind
and you moved the walls of my soul
even though I was used to armor
even though I had the protected shield activated
I had barriers up for I had seen the type before
and what you are capable of
but you came to me as a sheep
you came under the pretense of shyness
acted malleable,
you listened intently like you were definite.
just when I told the guards that they were no longer needed,
you showed me, did you show me.
you became a wolf
vicious, mean and lacking
you hunted me and attacked my soul

you forgot what you promised
your eyes became slits
you were beastly
uncaring
and off
you left like a wolf
with my heart in your fangs.

Unexpected

Out of nowhere
unexpected
not anticipated
I was alone
but connected
contented
not a possibility of movement
staying
no real longing
unaware that something might be missing
living, daily living
outsiders viewing me as
having all
me, believing I did
one day…
faithful day
all of a sudden
you.
you entered
without a knock.
I saw you walking up
I tried to lock my doors
I put barriers up
and closed windows and shades
I winterized my heart
hovered in corners
hiding from you
I handcuffed myself to others
and sealed all—airless
I wanted no air to seep in.
and just peeked out.
You never knocked

you kicked the door in
and once I looked
looked directly into your eyes
the house started to crumble
doors unlocked
shades opened
barriers moved and stored
melting
falling down
begging
changed me
so much movement
unchained I visualized
and looked outside
not just living but breathing, breathing, breathing
changing my clothes
empowered
wide open
and you came from nowhere
unexpected
and you never knew what you provided
with just one look

I Challenge You

to stay…
always and forever
forever
steady
ringed
committed
fresh
un-wanting
loving
kind
sweetly happy
gracefully age
always connected
longing for one another,
only
only you
only me.
him for you
she for him
unmovable
untouchable
committed indefinably
focused upon
developing
with kindness
and softness
fighting for love
airtight
and sealed
attacking outsiders
staying true
I challenge you to do.

Your New Woman Said I Rolled My Eyes at Her

Just because we used to be a we
does not mean I am holding a torch for you endlessly.
The assumptions that are presumed by you
are quite wrong
and I might add vain.
Just because you found someone new
years have passed since I wished there could be anything
between us
but here you are with your chest out
assuming and presuming things that you shouldn't.
What makes you feel that I still feel in that way for you?
I did not feel in that way for you when we were we.
I moved on and for women,
me,
moving on means getting on and putting feelings to rest.
Many relationships...
after you,
better than you
deeper than you
more loving than you,
sexier than you
kinder than you
more emotional than you
made a connection deep connection that I never made with
you.
So do not flatter yourself
you think too greatly of yourself
maybe you just want me to care
care about you,
love you and be with you
I have been over you
so don't be thinking that a torch is held
that fire went out a long time ago.

Step Forward, Move Back

You keep coming to me half way
You take a forward step,
then stumble back ways
I get excited,
hopeful…
I start to long for you,
even expect you.
Waiting for every tiny step,
perhaps you are really moving towards,
towards me, towards us.
coming back to me
you come forward and I wait.
and start to remember,
to dream of you,
of how we once touched,
of how your embrace felt
I sink into you, the memories.
I start to make plans,
I start moving to you,
hopeful that the itch will be scratched,
my hunger will be seized,
my body will be clothed,
my glass filled,
my soul reunited with its mate,
but then you step back,
and again I am crushed.

On My Knees

I have fallen on my knees,
no restraint,
no pride,
pride less,
without honor
or
dignity
begging you to approach
and stay with me.
begging you to come back,
to reconsider,
asking for the explanation on why…
why we can't be?
Why you left me behind?
Oh my, how I hurt,
stabbing pains that surround my heart,
but still down on my knees.

Full Libra

Diplomatic
and urbane
Romantic and charming
and sociable
Idealistic
Indecisive and changeable
Flirtatious
and self-indulgent
Venus is my ruler
I live that goddess.
Inanimate sign of the zodiac
Good taste
Lover of beauty, harmony
Artistic rather than intellectual
Good perception and observation
And with critical ability, with which I am able
To view my own efforts as well as those of others
I have integrity.
With my personal relationships,
I understand and compromise,
I allow claims against me to be settled to my own
disadvantage,
Rather than spoil a relationship.
I like the opposite sex a lot
To the extent of promiscuity sometimes,
And may indulge in romanticism bordering on sentimentality.
But I am good with marriages,
As along as it is a union of "true minds."
This is a Libra
This is me

Mr. Boulder-Dash

Enter your proxy
I spied across the jam-packed showcase
I slowed, creeping
Creeping
Creeping
I had an apparition
I anticipated
even had expectations of what I needed
I was delicate,
and unsophisticated
softly I crept
ever, so softly
I walked towards
your replacement
I stopped along the way,
inspecting others
other possible replacements,
not what was needed, wanted
so I continued toward
Mr. Dash.
I was careful not to make contact
with others
for I had respect for your replacement
I saw
beige ones
Tall and lean kinds
Purple
Rubber
and even glass,
but then I came upon it,
I knew I would take it home

and when I did
no more tension,
debating,
arguing
missing
and wanting...
I had pleasure without you.
you were replaced with a toy...
the toy resembled you.

Extra Credit

Okay,
you come home
and do not hang out with the boys
and you do not get high
and drink to the extreme
don't hang out in bars
and strip clubs
you do not have affairs
and you are loyal
the man takes care of his kids
and only has a few baby mamas'
pays child support
and cheers his children on,
sometimes he cooks dinner
and makes love to you so good.
he is strong,
Healthy,
Faithful,
Compromising,
Playful
Intense
Talented,
Flexible
And loving
He pays attention to you,
Asks about your day
Thoughtful gifts from him always
Indulges your pleasures.
He maintains a good job
and protects and honors you
he handles his business.
Well my friend that is what a man is supposed to do…
You get no extra credit for doing the right thing!

No Excuses

for me
who I am
what I have become
what I have been
the space that is needed
the air time required
the solo in my crowded life
my need to soar
to beat my chest
and stick it out
to leave you.
to meet new lovers
and make new friends
to be me
on my very own
I have no excuses
though you were very kind
and mended me in many ways
helped me, lifted me
supported me and indulged me…
to stay would be to take advantage
to stay would be selfish
for you deserve better,
you deserve complete love
you deserve the fantasy, the honesty
and I can no longer help you,
I have to help myself
and upon my exit,
I will make no excuses.

Deficient

Bottomless
Endless
Glass filled
Ocean wide
Spectacular
Relentless
Steadfast
for my blood connections
bending backwards
walking across hot rocks
Sheltering from harm
lean and bending
For my mother, sister, daughter, nieces, grandmother
brother,
maybe because I must,
I must be.
but for my love connections
my romantic liaisons,
my boyfriend,
my lover,
my husband
my connection to the opposite sex
made by destiny,
I always have my fill
and my heart exits.

We Will Never Be Friends

So here I sit.
We just had our interlude,
and conversed,
as if we might be converted into friends.
How do I begin to explain how unachievable that would be
for me
You have crept so profoundly into my interior
in spite of how much time has past,
you are with me indefinitely,
I yearn, no I pray that it would dissipate
But you just seep deeper into my soul
And there is no escape.
For you, perhaps, friendship could be pursued
for maybe, it wasn't so profound and there was no seeping
Perhaps, I wasn't what you are to me,
and oh, how that realization hurts down to the core
I can't be your pal, for the feelings are so beyond friendship
It is spiritual, life long, perpetual.
The truth that it might have been merely one-sided
distresses me,
for my keen judgment was off kilter, I a fool.
The deception is baffling.
To scrutinize your eyes as we spoke,
and for me to feel your presence and wait for a sign
Then the walk away, without even wanting to touch me,
The hug that lacked an embrace,
Oh, how it hurts
I hurt, I ache.
Tears that would not spill
Burned my eyes.
I felt a sock to my abdomen

A swift shock to my psyche
Perhaps we will meet again and perchance we might be friends,
But for me now I can not see it, for I want so much more than your friendship,
I want you inter-connected with me,
I want your eyes to penetrate the way mine do
Leaving you after our long separation has helped you to move passed me,
Leaving you after our long separation just reassured me of my feelings for you
There is the difference, I love you...truly love you
So here I sit, pondering the meeting,
Knowing that I will not meet you again,
I am not strong enough
Not strong enough, too damn weak,
to be your friend.

In the Car

Traumatized
aching and burning,
with soreness,
after our meeting.
I tried not to let them plummet
Be unresponsive
And hell, I should have been,
so much time passed,
and it should be all done
Finished,
I should be totally untouched,
But hurt just knocked on the door,
And I opened it.
I was the one who requested...
See me I asked,
See me I begged
See me, see me
Please see me
We can be friends,
No touching,
Absolutely no touching,
And it was easy for you,
Like I never mattered
And you gave me twenty minutes
Twenty fucking minutes
And you could barely spare that,
You nearly fell asleep
I am an idiot,
I am fool
To contemplate such foolish thoughts
So you walked away,

I called after you,
Still pleading,
And asked were you just finished with me?
You shook your head,
What the fuck was that?
And I sat
In the car
And willed myself not to shed,
Do not let them fall,
Sit up straight
And pretend that you are not affected,
Pretend that you are great,
And normal,
And untouched
And at that point, I questioned me
Weak and fragile me,
Still so moved by you,
You with all your indifference to me
In the car
My tears betrayed me
I cried again I cried,
But I believe a part of me
Finally let you go.

If You Loved Me

If you loved me and left me in spite of that said love
Then you are a Punk.
Yes, I said it
And I believe it to be so,
For if you loved me,
You couldn't leave
You wouldn't leave
You would fight,
Requested a dual
A match
Take me.
No matter what the barriers,
You would fight for me,
Rescue me,
Find the glass slipper,
Take me from whatever, whoever
No matter who stood guard,
Who ever was at the palace doors
You would break through
Run up the stairs
Scale the wall,
Go across the mote
Swim the channel
And take me,
But, only if you loved me,
So if I believed that I was not just one of those things
And that I was special,
For that is what you implied,
No, if memory serves me…you said.
Then you acted as a punk and never fought
Never asked the wicked step mother for my pardon,

Never kissed me,
Never fought for me.
What fairy tale ends with you saying...?
Well I love you so much,
But I will not battle for you.
You punked out
and no prince does that,
so I guess you are not my Prince Charming
you just pretended to be.

Crazy, Crazy

they should have put me away
why they did not, I will never understand
with such clarity I remember
what I was like
how I behaved
How I thought of you
and how you slapped me emotionally.
Men should have come in white suits
they should have restrained me
asked if I was okay
for with some examination
one would realize that I was not
that I was Crazy, Crazy

Did You Find Someone New?

Is she younger than I?
Skinner Than me?
less talkative
less needy
was I not smart enough?
was the distance too far
was I out of reach?
I need to know
Is she pretty?
with nice teeth
does she leave you breathless,
is she just not me, me, me?
do you say the same things you used to say to me?
touch her the way you touched me,
pull her in the way you pulled me in,
I am rejected,
insane with envy
needy
and still wanting
and waiting for you,
but it appears,
that you found someone new.

Porridge

The fire is on medium
The spices set aside
She stirs the pot,
it is steaming.
it smells of rich vanilla
nutmeg
warmed milk
maple syrup
and rosewood perfumed air
reaches my nose.
I watch her while I sit in the chair,
old and rough chair
I feel the wood
and know it is solid oak
not like my chairs,
cold and sterile.
she adds milk
three different kinds
condense,
evaporated
and fresh milk
and stirs
and mixes
and adds a pinch of salt,
and brown sugar
and I am lost
I wait
I feel transformed
to another time
when I was fresh
new

my small hands
wanting to stir with her,
too hot she would shout
and I would sit back
and wait
time has passed and I am here again
opened
ragged
scratched and bruised
with wisdom
her wisdom even more than mine
me, never catching up
her hands now have brown spots
but are still sturdy
she serves me,
as she did when my hands were small
and I am transformed

Red Snapper

not blue
or yellow
but red
Friday
in my mother's home
I would journey
reposition
stumble and falter
brush myself off
and continue on my way
for today is the day
and when I arrive,
I will always get
what I long for
to intake the aroma
and the view of.
she used to try and trick me
and serve me
yellow,
or blue
or even white
saying it was red
but I always knew
I have arrived in
old, freshly painted and
brand new cars
with my friends,
my family,
some associates and even foes
but I never stopped longing
to be home

and go to the market
to watch her barter
asking to keep the heads
which I never ate
then she would prepare for me
with her loving hands
my sides: Boiled banana, Dumplings and salad
hot and spicy red snapper with tomatoes and onion
and the taste was superior
because it came from my mothers hands

Cool

Front Faced, eyes direct, chest vertical,
Deliberate but almost languid movement
with a subtle dip
favoring right side
you tread...
long legged
deep chocolate, auburn, tamed tan, with some mocha.
I slant back and relax to see
that complex emotion that is erupted in me
it isn't tangible,
no amount of study would allow one to achieve,
it is crisp and connected only to you.
With each step forward, I watch you.
You: a bit presumptuous.
I shade my eyes
willing myself to reverse
DO NOT MOVE FORWARD,
come down some degrees
but I am preheated and it just doesn't happen.
forbidden, yet attainable
temptation, frustration and aggravation with oneself,
with this apprehensive desire
all from...a stride, your stride
a certain something, just something.
right there, unmistakable, yet not recognizable.
clandestine, forbidden and very sexy,
some kind of nothing that is magnificent
I am so inclined
to watch, to take hold, to touch and handle.
A portrait is blazed into my psyche
· I will rewind and play them later

The picture of you will hold in my memory,
I will hear the voice of man,
husky: colored richly brown
almost how deep dark chocolate would sound
if it had a voice.
all of this and you are unaware, just in attendance.
Just thinking of it, makes me warm.

Happy Birthday

Yes I remembered
How could I forget?
or did you think that because you forgot to remember
when my own birthday took place, that I would forget yours.
Unfortunately it doesn't play like that,
I remember you,
so I remember important days in your life
I think of you all day long,
so forget, I would not
I actually wish I could,
but no, I always know.
I am glad that you moved on
and that you are contented
I can say the content, goes both ways,
but I haven't taken a single step forward
as a matter of fact.
I am right where you left me
for a while I was a deer in high beams
unable to move,
then I moved in a trance like state
but I moved only in actions that others could see
inside I stood there in the same spot
longing and hoping that you might look back
you didn't and I waited
it was uneventful,
so you asked me about your birthday
Well I can't forget
So Happy Birthday Love.

Wake Me

When I slumber, you must wake me
As I lay in a deep penetrating sleep
Wake me.
I decide to lay me down and I always do the same
I wander and I drift,
I drift and fall
Wake me
Do not assume that I want to slumber even though I look
transformed.
Peaceful in my solitude
so far away from REM
and blissfully at rest
Wake me!
Regardless of how much you must upset your not so placid
rest
YOU NEED TO WAKE ME!
Even though unspoken words say leave me
and actions say leave me
you should just make the assumption
and Wake me.
I may be far below where you lay,
no matter the time or the flights you need to take
or how you must distress
or where you lay your head
you should and must Wake me.
Selfish you may say,
not so I say
for you are responsible for my unyielding neck
my aching posterior,
my sleeping practice.
For you allowed me to develop this blueprint…

allowed me these comforts
led me to where I am,
where I have traveled,
you should Wake me.
It is your responsibility
to be responsible for me
You should Wake me.

Where is the Love Letter?

A letter,
No not an email
Or a note on a post-it
Write me a letter, a love letter
A love note
On a card,
Or fine stationary
With your name embossed
And fine paper
Thinly cut
And of superior quality
Describe how you feel,
And ask how I feel about you.
You shouldn't type it,
It should be handwritten,
Special hearts
Do not hold back
Woo me, like the old fashioned books describe.
Express yourself proudly without pretense.
Write and say it in marker or pen—permanent thoughts
Salutations,
Beginnings
Summaries
Express never ending love
And forever passion
And closings
The closing with love deeply expressed
mail it, with a stamp...please

Polaris

The North Star

I have become fascinated with this star
and it's lack of movement in the sky.
my navigational tool
charting my path.
After you pointed it out
you became part of my focus
and the star was in full view
I had not noticed before, until you
You showed me the most magnificent light
and I have been following you in my heart
My heart that was opened by you
and the chemical pull between you and I

brightest star in the constellation the Little Dipper,
you taught me to follow that to find you
it is no wonder Polaris appears to be fixed
and all other stars and constellations seem to
revolve around the North Star...I worry

For you are imprinted inside my sky
I can not look up without thinking of you
and if the night is clear and the midnight sky is that exact color
of navy
I am fixed and transformed back to where it began
back to you.

I have been trying to find Polaris in the sky
I locate the Big Dipper as we once did together
your arms so inviting.

and follow the two stars at the end of the basin upward
I soon look away to wipe the tears that are flowing from my
eyes
once my vision is clear, I return to my learned behavior
I locate Polaris and remember with joy that you said
"It is the last star in the tail of the Little Dipper"

And a powerful pull says "you are my true North"
The feelings brought forth by you has forever changed me,
I know what I want, what I can not accept and what I should
feel.
My North of the South is you.

And So I Go

go to where I should have been
I surrender to lost endeavors
relinquish commitments
The meaning finally summarized
my being free
unrestricted
without restraint
I go
I run endlessly
without regret
the sequence of events,
the rapture ended.
do not look at me with sad eyes
you know that they hold me
and I am obliged to go,
for I am not really here with you
in this time, in your space
I am not happy caged
breathing has become a necessity
and I need water to help me grow
showers and sun
don't watch me walk
turn from me quickly…
and do not try and stop me
do not beg,
or make wishes upon stars
for that would just hold me for a little while
and how unfair would that be
know that when I was here,
I was really and truly here.
But now I am no longer with you

there has been a disconnection
cord broken beyond repair
do not despair
for you will be well
just let me go
this is was is destined to be
you with you
and me with me

Printed in the United States
46301LVS00002B/88-198